Little Princesses
The Snowflake Princess

By Katie Chase

Illustrated by Leighton Noyes

Red Fox

Special thanks to Narinder Dhami

THE SNOWFLAKE PRINCESS
A RED FOX BOOK 978 0 099 48832 3 (from January 2007)
0 099 48832 9

First published in Great Britain by Red Fox,
an imprint of Random House Children's Books

This edition published 2006

1 3 5 7 9 10 8 6 4 2

Series created by Working Partners Ltd
Copyright © Working Partners Ltd, 2006
Illustrations copyright © Leighton Noyes, 2006
Cover illustration by Nila Aye

Papers used by Random House Children's Books are natural, recyclable products
made from wood grown in sustainable forests. The manufacturing processes conform
to the environmental regulations of the country of origin.

Set in 15/21pt Bembo Schoolbook

Red Fox Books are published by Random House Children's Books,
61–63 Uxbridge Road, London W5 5SA,
a division of The Random House Group Ltd,
in Australia by Random House Australia (Pty) Ltd,
20 Alfred Street, Milsons Point, Sydney, NSW 2061, Australia,
in New Zealand by Random House New Zealand Ltd,
18 Poland Road, Glenfield, Auckland 10, New Zealand,
and in South Africa by Random House (Pty) Ltd,
Isle of Houghton, Corner Boundary Road & Carse O'Gowrie,
Houghton 2198, South Africa

THE RANDOM HOUSE GROUP Limited Reg. No. 954009
www.**kids**at**randomhouse**.co.uk

A CIP catalogue record for this book is available from the British Library.

Printed and bound in Great Britain by
Cox & Wyman Ltd, Reading, Berkshire

For Elodie, with love to Mummy and
Daddy's pet monkey
L.N.

For Janet and Louisa Haslum
M.H.

Chapter One

What's that noise? Rosie wondered, frowning.

She stopped dusting the carved wooden fireplace and slowly turned round. She was sure she'd heard something rattling behind her. She listened hard. There it was again! But there was no one in the huge dining room except herself.

Rosie put the pink feather duster down on the enormous polished dining table. It was Christmas Eve and her eyes were drawn to the giant Christmas tree that stood in the Great Hall. The tree was decorated with glittering baubles and shiny tinsel, and it sparkled with fairy lights. But Rosie couldn't see anyone around.

She turned back and picked up her feather duster again. Like the rest of the castle, the dining room was crammed with beautiful treasures and antiques, collected by Rosie's Great-aunt Rosamund on her many travels around the world. In one corner of the room stood a suit of shining silver armour. Rosie glanced at it, and her eyes widened in alarm; one arm was slowly moving upwards . . .

Then she guessed what was going on. "Luke!" Rosie shouted, hurrying across the room. "Come out of there!"

Luke, Rosie's younger brother, popped out from behind the armour, and grinned cheekily at her. "Did I scare you?" he asked hopefully.

"No, you didn't," Rosie replied with a smile. "Didn't Mum tell you to tidy your room?"

Luke pulled a face. "I've *nearly* finished," he said.

Rosie used the feather duster to tickle Luke on the nose. "Mum'll be after you," she teased. "You know she wants the castle looking its best when Aunt Sally and Uncle Mark arrive for Christmas."

Luke nodded and ran out of the dining room. "I hate tidying up," he shouted as he went. "But I love living in Great-aunt Rosamund's castle. And I *love* Christmas!"

Rosie smiled to herself. She had been thrilled when Great-aunt Rosamund had asked Rosie and her family to come and live in her Scottish castle while she went travelling for two years. The castle wasn't quite the same without her great-aunt around, but Rosie had soon discovered that Great-aunt Rosamund had left her a special message, and it revealed an amazing secret. Hidden around the castle were lots of little princesses for Rosie to find. And whenever Rosie found one, a wonderful adventure always followed.

Rosie went back to her dusting. Her family usually ate their meals in the kitchen, but since it was Christmas and they were having visitors, they were going to eat in the dining room for the very first time.

It was an impressive room. The large wooden table was surrounded by twelve chairs with red velvet-padded seats. On its polished surface stood several gleaming silver candlesticks and a large vase of white lilies.

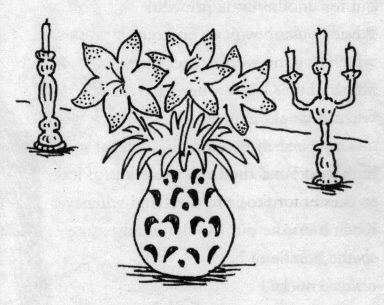

Long, red velvet curtains hung at the arched windows, tied back with twisted gold ropes. And the shelves on either side of the great fireplace were packed with treasures like tiny silver boxes, decorated china eggs, old leather-bound books and carved wooden animals.

Rosie began to dust the shelves carefully. Wherever she went in the castle, she was always on the look-out for another little princess. Rosie couldn't wait to find out which one she would meet next, but she never knew where and when it would happen.

The top shelf was quite high, and Rosie had to stand on tiptoe to reach it. As she did so, the handle of her duster knocked against something on the shelf and sent it flying.

"Oh, no!" Rosie gasped in horror. She made a grab at

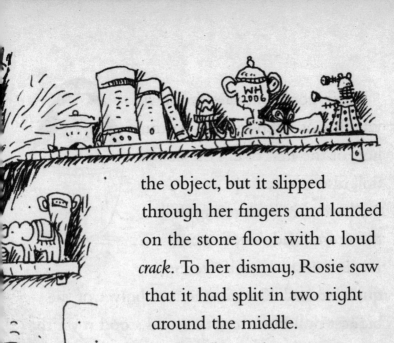

the object, but it slipped
through her fingers and landed
on the stone floor with a loud
crack. To her dismay, Rosie saw
that it had split in two right
around the middle.

Her heart thumping,
Rosie quickly dropped the
duster and knelt down to see if
she could fix it. She picked up the
two halves, and smiled with relief.
It's a Russian doll! she
thought, holding the two
wooden pieces, one in each
hand. It's supposed to come
apart. There's another doll
inside it.

Rosie took out the second doll, which was sitting in the bottom half of the first one. The second doll also opened up.

"I wonder how many dolls there are inside each other," Rosie said to herself, feeling quite excited. She put the two halves of the biggest doll back together and stood it on the polished table. The doll was brightly painted, wearing a rich, blue velvet robe and a golden crown.

"I think this first one's a king," Rosie murmured, staring at the doll's jet-black hair and small, pointed beard. She picked up the second doll. "And this one's a queen."

The second doll wore a glittering golden tiara and a

flowing dress of ruby-red silk. Rosie opened it up, took out a third doll and stood the queen on the table next to the king.

The third doll was a man dressed in a black velvet gown spangled with silver moons and stars. He had a long white beard, and carried a shining silver wand. Rosie decided that he must be a magician and stood him next to the queen.

Inside the magician was yet another smaller doll. This one was wearing a white shirt, baggy black trousers and a furry hat. From his fierce expression, Rosie concluded that he must be a warrior. He had a leather scabbard hanging at his side, with a sword in it.

How many more are there? Rosie

wondered, as she took the warrior apart and another doll appeared. This one was a young man, as richly dressed as the king and queen, in purple velvet and white silk. He also had a small golden crown on his dark hair.

A prince, Rosie decided. She peered closely at the doll, and saw that there was a crack around the middle. Oh, I think there's one more . . .

Rosie unscrewed the two halves of the prince, and a tiny doll fell out and rolled a little way across the shiny surface of the table. Quickly Rosie put the prince back together and stood him beside the warrior.

"I've got a king, a queen, a magician, a warrior and a prince," Rosie said with a smile. She reached across the table to pick up the last and smallest doll. "I wonder what this one will be?"

Rosie stared down at the tiny doll lying in

her hand. It was a girl, wearing a long red dress trimmed with white fur. A tiny golden tiara sat on her flowing blonde hair. But her pretty painted face looked rather unhappy.

Rosie's heart began to beat faster as excitement flooded through her. "It's a little princess!" she gasped, hardly able to believe her eyes.

Her hand shaking, Rosie stood the little princess on the table next to the prince. Then, following the instructions in her Great-aunt Rosamund's secret message, she dipped into a low curtsey. "Hello!" she said breathlessly, her eyes fixed on the tiny princess doll.

No sooner had the words left

her lips than Rosie felt an icy wind sweep into the room. The whirlwind immediately wrapped itself around her, and Rosie saw tiny, sparkling snowflakes dancing in the breeze. The whirlwind became stronger, and as it gently lifted her off the ground, Rosie could hear the faint sound of jingling bells. She closed her eyes, wondering where the whirlwind was taking her. She couldn't wait to find out!

Chapter Two

A few moments later, Rosie felt her feet land
on something soft. When she opened her eyes,
she gave a gasp of amazement.

She was surrounded by deep snow, as far
as the eye could see. The countryside was
covered with a thick blanket of white that
sparkled in the sunlight, making the trees
and fields look as if they had been frosted
with sugar. Not far away, Rosie could see a
great forest of tall pine trees. Glittering snow
lined their branches, making them look like
giant decorated Christmas trees. Beyond the
forest, Rosie could see a range of enormous

mountains whose snowy peaks stretched towards the clouds.

I wonder where I am, she thought, puzzled.

Glancing down at herself, Rosie realized that she was now wearing a warm cloak of scarlet wool, with a hood that fastened snugly under her chin. Although it was so cold that Rosie could see her breath, she actually felt quite cosy.

As Rosie was admiring her pretty cloak, she suddenly heard the sound of jingling bells in the distance. She looked up, and to her great excitement, saw a sleigh drawn by two white horses speeding across the snow towards her.

"Oh!" Rosie gasped. "A real sleigh! I've never seen one before!"

The sleigh was painted a bright red, and the sides were decorated with gold and silver patterns. Tiny silver bells hung from the sleigh and from the horses' reins, and they jingled merrily as the sleigh sped along on its silver runners.

Inside the sleigh, seated on red velvet cushions, was a young girl holding the horses' reins.

She wore a scarlet cloak like Rosie's with the hood up, but as she drew the horses to a stop, she pushed the hood back. Her long blonde hair tumbled out, and Rosie's eyes opened wide. She recognized the girl. She was the smallest doll, the little princess!

The little princess looked at Rosie, and her face lit up in a big smile. Tossing the reins aside, she scrambled out of the sleigh.

"Oh, I'm so glad to see you!" she announced, giving Rosie a big hug. "I'm Princess Anastasia, and I've been so lonely!" Then she frowned. "But what are you doing out here all alone? How did Baba Yaga miss you?"

Rosie looked confused. "I don't know who

Baba Yaga is," she replied. "My name's Rosie. And I'm here because—"

"Rosie?" Looking amazed, Princess Anastasia clapped a hand to her mouth. "Oh! You must be my magic friend who's come to help!"

"I think I am!" replied Rosie with a smile, remembering what had happened in her previous adventures.

Anastasia was nodding excitedly. "Every Christmas Day I would always sit in front of the fire with my grandmother and she would tell me stories about her own magic friend, who used to visit her whenever she needed help," Anastasia explained. "Her name was Rosamund."

"That's my Great-aunt Rosamund!" laughed Rosie. "But where are we?"

"In Russia," Anastasia replied, waving her hand at the snowy countryside around them.

"My father and mother are the tsar and tsarina."

"The king and queen?" Rosie guessed.

The princess nodded.

"So why do you need my help?" asked Rosie curiously.

Anastasia's pretty face fell. "Oh, Rosie," she sighed. "Something terrible has happened. Six days ago the evil witch Baba Yaga burst into our Christmas ball, and cast a spell on my family. My parents and all the royal court have been turned to ice! Baba Yaga has ruined Christmas!"

Chapter Three

Rosie could hardly believe her ears. "*Everyone* has been turned to ice?" she repeated.

"Everyone," Anastasia confirmed sadly, "except me."

"How did you manage to escape?" asked Rosie.

Anastasia shook her head. "I didn't," she replied. "Baba Yaga won't freeze me because she wants to collect my tears."

Rosie stared at the princess in astonishment. "Why?" she gasped.

"Baba Yaga collects the tears of young girls, and uses them in her magic spells to

make herself look young and beautiful,"
explained Anastasia. "If it wasn't for her
magic, she'd be dead by now. She's at least
two hundred years old!"

"That's *really* old!" Rosie exclaimed.

"Baba Yaga wants to look young again
more than anything," Anastasia went on.
"She's taken all the mirrors from the royal
palace to her own house, just so that she can
look at herself all day while she mixes spells
to make herself more beautiful."

"She sounds
horrible," Rosie said
with a shudder.

"She is,"
Anastasia agreed,
her eyes filling
with tears. "I miss
my family so
much. It's very

lonely in the palace on my own."

"Where's Baba Yaga now?" Rosie asked, glancing over her shoulder rather nervously.

"In her tree house in the heart of the Great Forest," Anastasia replied, pointing across the frozen waste at the pine trees in the distance. "I'm just glad Baba Yaga didn't freeze me too," she went on, drying her tears. "Because at least I have a chance to save my family and release them from the spell, if only I can find a way!"

"I'll help you!" Rosie said quickly. "Together we must be able to come up with something."

Anastasia took Rosie's hand. "Let's go back to the palace, and I'll show you what happened to my family," she suggested. "Then maybe we can come up with a plan."

The two girls went over to the sleigh, where the white horses were waiting patiently for them. Anastasia helped Rosie to climb aboard. Then she sat down, tucked a snowy-white blanket around their knees, and picked up the reins.

Rosie snuggled down under the blanket as the horses moved off, quickly picking up speed as they broke into a brisk trot. The sleigh skimmed so quickly and smoothly over the snow that Rosie felt as if they were almost flying through the air.

"Look, Rosie," Anastasia said after a few minutes. "There's the royal palace ahead."

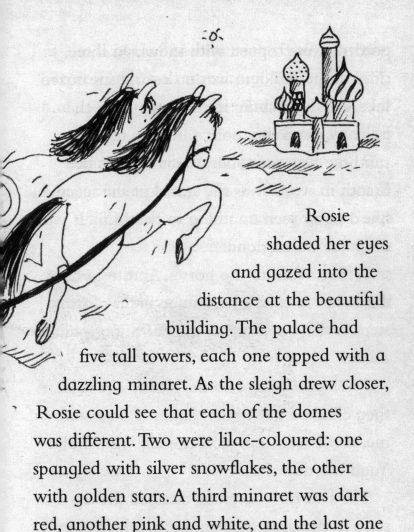

Rosie
shaded her eyes
and gazed into the
distance at the beautiful
building. The palace had
five tall towers, each one topped with a
dazzling minaret. As the sleigh drew closer,
Rosie could see that each of the domes
was different. Two were lilac-coloured: one
spangled with silver snowflakes, the other
with golden stars. A third minaret was dark
red, another pink and white, and the last one
was striped with green and gold.

Like everywhere else, the palace and the

gardens were topped with snow. On three sides of the building was an enormous frozen lake, and long shiny icicles hung from the balconies and the roofs, glittering in the sunshine like diamonds. Rosie caught her breath in wonder as she stared at the scene. She'd never seen anything so beautiful. It was a winter wonderland.

With a word to the horses, Anastasia drew the sleigh to a halt by a huge flight of stone steps which swept up to the enormous palace doors.

"Welcome to my home, Rosie," she said, as they climbed out of the sleigh. "Come with me, and I will show you exactly what Baba Yaga has done."

The two girls carefully climbed the icy steps to the great golden doors, which stood ajar. Rosie followed Anastasia inside, and then stopped to stare in amazement.

They were standing in a grand entrance
hall with a sweeping marble staircase.
Everything was very grand, but it was all
encased in sheets of sparkling ice. Rosie could
see icicles hanging from the banisters of the

staircase and from the tops of the windows. It
was just as cold inside as it was outside.

Rosie spun around slowly, staring at the
icy hall. "This is terrible!" she breathed.

"I know," Anastasia sighed. "And there's
worse to come. This way." She led Rosie over
to another set of doors.

"This is the ballroom," Anastasia explained as she pushed the doors open. "We were in the middle of the Christmas ball when Baba Yaga arrived."

Rosie stepped into the ballroom and gazed around in wonder. The room was full of people wearing exquisite silk, satin and velvet clothes, and all of them were covered with a frosting of glittering ice. Many of them had been caught by the spell as they were dancing, frozen for ever as they whirled and spun around the room. Above their heads hung crystal chandeliers, now completely encased in shimmering ice, and in the middle of the room stood the biggest Christmas tree Rosie had ever seen. It was beautifully decorated with glass birds that glittered with jewels, and a dazzling star at the top that shone as if it were made of pure gold. But the whole tree was now covered in ice, and icicles hung, sparkling, from every branch.

"I can't believe this!" Rosie murmured, gazing around the frozen ballroom.

"The Christmas ball is the grandest celebration of the year," Anastasia told her. "And it always takes place exactly seven days before Christmas Day. This year's ball was particularly special," she went on, "because we were also celebrating my brother's engagement." Anastasia pointed past the dancers to a raised platform at the front of the ballroom. "That's my brother, Prince Alexei, and his bride-to-be, Irina."

A young man with a gold crown on his dark head sat on a carved throne upon the platform. Rosie looked more closely and recognized the prince from the set of Russian dolls. He was holding the hand of a pretty dark-haired girl in an emerald-green dress. Both of them were encased in ice. Near them

was an orchestra, all the musicians frozen
with their instruments still in their hands.
Anastasia began to thread her way carefully
through the dancers, and Rosie followed. It
felt very strange to be walking past frozen
people who didn't seem to know that they
were there.

"This is my mother and father," Anastasia said sadly, her hand trembling as she pointed at one of the couples frozen while they danced.

Rosie saw that the tsar and tsarina looked exactly like the two biggest Russian dolls, although their richly coloured clothes were now covered with sparkling ice. In front of them stood a man with a fierce expression on his face, his sword half drawn from its scabbard.

"The warrior!" Rosie gasped.

"Yes, that is Ivan Ivanovitch, my parents' guard," explained Anastasia. "He was drawing his sword to protect them at the very moment Baba Yaga cast her spell." She turned to the tall thin man with a long white beard who stood next to the warrior. "And this is Nikolai, our court magician."

Rosie stared at the magician, also one

of the dolls she had seen back at the castle. His wand was raised and a gleaming silver bolt of magic leaped from the end of it, like lightning frozen in mid-air.

"Nikolai tried to cast a spell to stop Baba Yaga," Anastasia told Rosie. "But she was too quick for him."

Rosie shivered, suddenly feeling a little scared. If the court magician and the warrior hadn't managed to defeat Baba Yaga, she must be a very powerful witch indeed.

Anastasia led Rosie across the ballroom, past a grandfather clock still ticking softly beneath its sheet of ice. At one side of the room was a long table, laden with plates of delicious food. But the bread, the meat and the fruits were all frosted with ice. Rosie noticed that even the once-blazing fire in the wide stone hearth had frozen solid, its golden flames now shining, not with fiery sparks, but with tiny snowflakes.

"Is the whole palace like this, Anastasia?" Rosie asked.

Before the princess could answer, a freezing wind suddenly swept through the ballroom, setting the icy chandelier swaying and rattling. In the blink of an eye, the temperature had plummeted, so that Rosie began to shiver in spite of her warm clothes.

Looking very frightened, Anastasia grabbed Rosie's hand. "Baba Yaga is coming!" she gasped. "Quick, Rosie, you must hide. If she finds you, she will turn you to ice!"

Chapter Four

Rosie was so scared, she could hardly move. "Where shall I hide?" she asked urgently, glancing all around. But she was standing in the middle of the room amongst the frozen dancers, and there seemed to be nowhere to go. The girls heard footsteps echoing along the icy corridor outside the ballroom; Baba Yaga was getting closer.

"I'll have to pretend to be one of the dancers!" Rosie whispered urgently to Anastasia. "Here, take my cloak."

Quickly Rosie shrugged off her cloak and handed it to her new friend. Underneath,

she was wearing a long
gown of rose silk
embroidered with
golden thread. But
Rosie had no time to
admire her dress. She
hurried over to one of
the male dancers and
stood opposite him,
copying the position of
one of the other ladies
by raising her arms
gracefully in the
air. Her face pale,
Anastasia bent
down, scooped up
some ice and quickly
sprinkled it over Rosie.

"This will help to fool Baba Yaga," she said
softly. "But you *must* stay as still as you can."

The next moment, Baba Yaga stalked into
the room, and Rosie
had to bite her lip
to stop herself from
gasping. The witch
was a little old
woman, wrapped
in dusty black
clothes, with a
long, sharp nose
and stringy grey
hair. Her skin
was gnarled
and wrinkled
like a
walnut
and

her eyes, which darted into every corner of the ballroom, were narrow and red and seemed to spit fire.

"Baba Yaga!" Anastasia rushed to meet the witch and stood in front of her, shielding Rosie from her gaze. "Please, I beg you, undo your spell and release my family."

Baba Yaga ignored her. "There's something different about the palace today," she said in a croaky voice. "What is it?" And she lifted her pointed nose and sniffed the air.

"Nothing," Anastasia replied quickly. "Everything is exactly the same."

"I am *never* wrong!" snapped Baba Yaga, and her eyes flashed red sparks. Pushing Anastasia aside, she began to walk around the ballroom, peering into the faces of the frozen dancers.

Rosie was absolutely terrified. She kept as still as she could and held her breath as

Baba Yaga drew closer. The witch stopped right next to Rosie, so close that Rosie could feel the witch's breath on her icy skin. But Baba Yaga was looking over Rosie's shoulder, staring at the dancers behind her.

Rosie was so cold, she was afraid that she would start shivering and give herself away.

But just then, a loud sob echoed around the ballroom. Anastasia had begun to cry, and tears were streaming down her face.

"Tears!" screeched Baba Yaga, her face breaking into a grin and revealing rotten teeth. "Precious tears!"

She dashed across the ballroom towards Anastasia, pulling a tiny glass bottle from her sleeve. Then she held the bottle close to the princess's face, catching the tears one by one as they fell. Rosie watched in amazement.

"Baba Yaga," Anastasia sniffed, as she struggled to stop crying, "it's Christmas – *please* release my family!"

"Give me more tears!" Baba Yaga howled, her face turning purple with rage.

Rosie longed to go and comfort her friend, but she didn't dare move a muscle. After a moment or two, Anastasia dried her eyes. That made Baba Yaga even more furious.

"I *might* release your family . . ." the witch murmured slyly.

Anastasia looked up at her hopefully.

"But if I do, it will be so many years from now that you will be *old!*" the witch spat cruelly. "So old your own parents will no longer recognize you!"

Chapter Five

What a horrible old woman! Rosie thought indignantly. Poor Anastasia. She watched anxiously as Anastasia's lip began to tremble, and she burst out crying again. Greedily, Baba Yaga collected the precious tears, then snapped the lid of the bottle closed.

"Thank you, Princess," she cackled as she stalked over to the doors. "Very soon I will be young and beautiful again; that's my Christmas present to myself!" And Baba Yaga went off down the corridor, her triumphant laughter echoing around the silent, icy palace.

"Rosie, are you all right?" Anastasia cried, rushing over to her friend. "You must be frozen!"

"I am," Rosie replied through chattering teeth. She shook the ice off her dress, and wrapped her cloak around herself, shivering from head to toe. "I thought Baba Yaga was going to find me."

"That's why I started crying," Anastasia explained. "I knew it would distract her." She put her arm around Rosie's shoulders. "Now, come with me. You need to warm up."

Anastasia led Rosie out of the ballroom and through a maze of marble corridors. Like everything else Rosie had seen so far, all the furniture, carpets and curtains were frozen solid.

"Where are we going?" she asked.

"To the kitchen," replied Anastasia. "There's a place there that isn't frozen. Here we are."

Anastasia stopped in front of a large wooden door and pushed it open. The kitchen was enormous. At one end of the room, everything was icy like the rest of the palace, including the cook and the servants, who had been frozen solid as they prepared the food. But at the other end, Rosie was delighted to see that a small fire burned in the stone hearth.

"Oh, that's better!" she gasped, rushing over to the comforting blaze.

"Baba Yaga lets me have a fire so that I

don't freeze," explained Anastasia. "I sleep in here because this is the warmest part of the palace." She pointed at a bundle of blankets in the corner. "I can cook on the fire too. Would you like something to eat?"

Rosie grinned and nodded. "I'm starving!" she exclaimed.

"Sit down," said Anastasia, drawing a

wooden stool up to the hearth. "I'll heat up some soup."

Rosie huddled in front of the fire, while Anastasia held a small pan over the orange flames. Soon a rich, warm smell filled the kitchen.

"What is it?" Rosie asked, as Anastasia poured the creamy broth into two china bowls and handed Rosie a spoon.

"It's a Russian soup called *solyanka*," Anastasia told her. "It can be made in lots of different ways, but this is my favourite, with mushrooms, cream and spices."

Rosie blew on a spoonful of soup, and then took a sip. "It's lovely!" she sighed, feeling a warm, comforting glow steal over her.

Both girls began to eat hungrily as they sat in front of the fire.

"You've seen how terrible Baba Yaga is, Rosie," Anastasia sighed, handing her friend a chunk of rye bread. "What am I going to do?"

"Is there *any* way to break the spell?" Rosie asked, as she gazed thoughtfully into the fire.

"Well, there *is* one way," Anastasia replied slowly. "Baba Yaga told me of it herself, but it's impossible. Absolutely impossible!"

"Tell me," Rosie said eagerly.

Anastasia put down her spoon. "Baba Yaga said that if I can show her two snowflakes in the palace that look identical, before the grandfather clock in the ballroom strikes midnight on Christmas Eve, then the spell will be broken and the palace will return to normal. However, if I fail, the second it becomes Christmas Day, Baba Yaga's magic will become permanent and then I will never be able to break the spell."

Rosie stared at her friend in dismay. "But everyone knows that no two snowflakes are the same! Every single one is different."

Anastasia nodded. "And today is Christmas Eve," she added. Tears sprang into her eyes. "The spell will *never* be broken and my friends and family will be frozen for ever!"

Rosie frowned. Baba Yaga had obviously set this cruel task believing that it was impossible for Anastasia to carry it out. But she felt there *had* to be a way ...

Suddenly Rosie sat up straight, her eyes gleaming with excitement. "Anastasia," she said eagerly, "I've got an idea!"

Chapter Six

"You have?" Anastasia stared at Rosie, her eyes wide. "What is it?"

"We'll need a mirror," Rosie began, but immediately Anastasia's face fell.

"Oh, Rosie," she sighed. "Don't you remember? Baba Yaga is so vain. She stole every mirror from the palace and took them to her tree house."

"What, all of them?" Rosie asked.

Anastasia nodded.

Rosie thought fast. "Then we'll have to go and get one of the mirrors back," she said firmly.

"Oh!" Anastasia stared at her. "Rosie, Baba Yaga lives right at the heart of the Great Forest. No one has ever been there – and certainly no one has *ever* managed to steal something from her!"

"Well, there's a first time for everything!" Rosie replied, trying not to look too scared herself. "We must have a mirror, or my plan won't work."

Anastasia took a deep breath. "All right," she said bravely. "I'll take you to Baba Yaga's house."

"Do you know the way?" Rosie asked, and Anastasia nodded.

"We set out from the lake and follow the river deep into the Great Forest," she explained. "Then we must walk through the trees until we reach the dark heart of the forest. That's where we'll find Baba Yaga's house. But we don't have much time," she added. "The river takes a long and winding route into the Great Forest, and we can't take a boat because the water is frozen. We shall have to skate."

"Ice-skate, you mean?" Rosie asked, looking alarmed. "I'm sorry, Anastasia, I don't know how."

"I'll teach you," Anastasia promised. "It isn't hard."

Rosie stood up. "Let's get started then," she said eagerly. "How much time do we have?"

"We must check the grandfather clock," Anastasia replied, hurrying over to the door.

Rosie followed her, and the two girls rushed back to the ballroom. As they entered the room, the clock was chiming nine.

"We have three hours until midnight," Anastasia said anxiously. She went over to a pair of French windows and pushed them open. Darkness had fallen, but the moon shone, bright and full, and stars glittered in the deep blue of the night sky. In the moonlight, Rosie could see the frozen lake stretching away, beyond the palace gardens, in the direction of the Great Forest.

"I'll fetch the skates, and we'll go down to the lake," Anastasia said. "Wait here, Rosie."

As Rosie waited for Anastasia to return, she couldn't help feeling a little nervous. What if she couldn't learn how to skate? Rosie had seen ice-skating on television, and she didn't think it looked very easy at all. But they *had* to journey to Baba Yaga's house and get a mirror before midnight, or Anastasia's family and all the people in the palace would be frozen for ever!

When Anastasia came back, Rosie felt
even more worried. The skates were made
of dark-brown leather and had large, heavy
blades. They looked nothing like the neat

white boots she'd seen
skaters wearing on TV.
"Quickly, Rosie."
Anastasia took her
hand, and together
they went out of
the French windows
and across the snowy
lawn towards the lake. There they sat down
on an iron bench, made into the shape
of a peacock's tail, and put the skates on.
Anastasia had brought a leather bag so that
they could take their shoes with them.

"Lace the skates very tightly," Anastasia
told Rosie. "Now, stand up and give me your
hands."

Rosie got cautiously to her feet. The boots
felt heavy and awkward as she hobbled onto
the frozen lake with Anastasia's help.

"Stand up tall and straight," Anastasia

advised Rosie, "and try not to look down at your feet."

Rosie could feel the blades of her skates digging into the ice, but she couldn't get her balance at all. She wobbled as she stood there, clinging desperately to Anastasia.

"Now turn your feet out," the princess told her.

"I can't," Rosie laughed. "I'm afraid I'll fall over if I move!"

"I'll hold onto you." Anastasia smiled. "Turn your feet out, bend your knees a bit and try gliding forward a little, one foot at a time. Don't make big movements at first."

Rosie did as she was told. "I'm moving!" she gasped as she edged forwards. "I'm wobbling, but I'm moving!"

Anastasia began to tow Rosie slowly around the edge of the lake. Although Rosie was unsteady on her feet at first, she gradually got her balance and found a rhythm.

"Now try on your own," Anastasia said, letting go of Rosie's hands.

Rosie struck out boldly and ended up sitting down on the ice with a thump.

Anastasia helped her up. "Try again," she laughed.

Rosie set out again, and this time she managed five steps before she tumbled over. She scrambled to her feet, and struck out once more.

Meanwhile, Anastasia skated backwards so that she could keep an eye on Rosie.

"You're brilliant," Rosie said enviously, as she climbed to her feet for the third time. She grinned as Anastasia did a few twirls, followed by a fast spin. "I wish I could do that."

"I've been skating since I could walk!" Anastasia said with a smile. "Come on, once more round the lake."

This time, Rosie managed

to stay on her feet as they skated round the lake. She even began to pick up a bit of speed.

"You're doing well," Anastasia said, smiling at Rosie's progress. "And I think we should set off for Baba Yaga's house now. Do you think you can make it, Rosie?"

"Of course I can!" Rosie said in a determined voice, trying not to wobble too much.

"It's that way," Anastasia said, pointing ahead of them at the river, which shone in the moonlight like a silver ribbon as it snaked away towards the Great Forest.

Rosie shivered, pulling up the hood of her cloak. "Let's go," she said bravely, taking Anastasia's hand.

Anastasia flung the bag with their shoes in it over her shoulder, and the two girls skated off across the lake towards the river. Soon they were flying along at quite a speed, the cold night wind turning their cheeks pink. The moon, high in the dark sky, bathed the pine trees of the Great Forest in a silvery light.

On the way, Rosie explained her plan to Anastasia. "Any snowflake reflected in a mirror, will look like *two identical snowflakes*," she pointed out. "If we show Baba Yaga, that will surely break her spell!"

"Oh, yes, Rosie," Anastasia agreed excitedly. "I think it will. Perhaps that's why Baba Yaga took all the mirrors away! But we have to find a mirror *and* get Baba Yaga back to the palace before midnight."

Rosie nodded. She was beginning to feel much more confident on skates now, especially with Anastasia holding her hand. As they sped along the river, she noticed that the trees were growing closer and closer

together. Soon they were so densely packed
that there wasn't even any snow on the
ground between them.

"This is the spring – the source of the
river," Anastasia said, as the river dwindled to
become a stream which sprang from amongst
a pile of rocks. "We'll have to walk the rest of
the way."

The girls glided to the edge of the river,
and removed their skates. Rosie's ankles
ached from the weight of the heavy boots,
and she was glad to slip her shoes on again.

"Which way do we go now?" she asked.

"Follow me," Anastasia replied, heading
into the dark forest.

The trees grew so closely together here
that the moonlight could hardly shine
through the branches, and it was hard for
the girls to see where they were going in the
gloom.

They walked for what seemed a very long time. Then, suddenly, a large tree, bigger than any Rosie had seen so far, loomed out of the darkness in front of them.

"That's Baba Yaga's tree house," whispered Anastasia.

Her heart thumping, Rosie gazed at the house. It was lit by torches from within, and she could see two large windows, like staring eyes, in the trunk. The door below them looked like a gaping mouth, and it was

hung with pointed icicles like vicious fangs.

Rosie glanced upwards and saw that the whole tree was hung with icicles too.

"The icicles are Baba Yaga's alarm system," Anastasia told Rosie. "It's famous throughout the land. If one icicle is knocked, it hits another and then another, until all the icicles are knocking and ringing together. We must be very careful not to knock into one, Rosie!"

Chapter Seven

Trying not to look scared, Rosie grinned at Anastasia. "Follow me," she said. "I think I know how we can get inside."

She bent and picked up a stone, and then the two of them crept towards the door of Baba Yaga's house. Rosie tried not to look at the sharp icicles as she knocked on the door, using the doorknocker, which was shaped like a skull. After a  moment, the two girls heard footsteps coming towards them from inside the house.

"Quick, Anastasia, hide behind that tree!"
Rosie said urgently.

They both hurried to hide behind the

nearest tree. The front
door opened, and an old
man with a long grey
beard looked out.

"That's Igor, Baba
Yaga's servant,"
Anastasia whispered
in Rosie's ear. "He
sometimes comes with
her to the palace."

Looking puzzled,
Igor scratched his head,
clearly wondering
why there was no one
around. He was about to go back inside
when Rosie suddenly tossed the stone away
into the undergrowth. It landed with a thud.

"Who's there?" Igor growled. Leaving the door open, he trudged away through the trees to take a look. As soon as he was out of sight, Rosie and Anastasia crept out from behind the tree and rushed into the house.

"We're in!" Rosie said triumphantly. "And it looks like we go this way."

Ahead of them was a long, dark tunnel which seemed to wind underground beneath the spreading roots of the tree. Rosie and Anastasia hurried down the tunnel. It was pitch-black and they couldn't see a thing.

"There's something glittering ahead of us," Anastasia whispered. "What is it?"

Rosie peered through the darkness. "I can see it too," she whispered back. "Oh!" Her eyes widened in amazement as they drew near the end of the tunnel. "It's *mirrors*! Lots of them."

The girls had come out into a large hall

lined with mirrors. The mirrors covered the walls, the ceiling and the floor. Many winding corridors led from the hall, deeper into the house, and the girls could see that each of these was lined with mirrors too.

"This one is from the palace," Anastasia said, pointing at a large, arched mirror in a gilt frame. "And this one, *and* this one," she added, recognizing a couple more.

"Are they all from the palace?" Rosie asked. "There are so many of them." She slowly spun round on her heel, staring at the mirrors. Hundreds of reflections of Rosie spun too.

Anastasia shook her head. "Baba Yaga must have collected these from all over the place."

"And made her very own giant hall of mirrors!" Rosie breathed.

"Let's take one and get out of here," said

Anastasia anxiously.

Rosie frowned. "But they're all really big," she said. "We can't carry any of these. We have to find something smaller."

Quickly the two girls searched the hall of mirrors. There were many different mirrors in a variety of gold, silver and wooden frames, but all of them were too large and heavy for the girls to carry.

"Baba Yaga *must* have some smaller mirrors," Rosie said. "We'll have to search the rest of the house."

"I've just remembered," Anastasia whispered suddenly. "Baba Yaga took my mother's silver hand mirror from her dressing table. It must be here somewhere."

"That sounds perfect," Rosie told her. "Let's look for it. We'll start down there." And she pointed at one of the mirror-lined corridors.

But Anastasia was looking worried. "Rosie, all these corridors look the same," she pointed out. "If we go deeper into the house, how will we ever find our way back to the front door?"

Rosie frowned and thought hard for a moment. Then her face brightened, and she began pulling at a loose thread in her scarlet cloak.

"What are you doing?" Anastasia asked curiously.

"Leaving a trail," Rosie replied, as the woollen thread came away.

Pulling the thread to make it longer, Rosie tied the end of it to a hook in the wall.

"We won't get lost in this maze of mirrors now," she announced. "As we go deeper into the house, my cloak will unravel, and we'll be able to follow the thread back to the door!"

"Good idea," Anastasia laughed, sounding impressed. "Now, let's hurry!"

The girls headed down one of the corridors, the scarlet thread unravelling behind them as they went. Soon they were very glad of it, for they were completely lost in the maze of mirrors.

Along the way they peered into various rooms. One contained a big black cauldron, full of a thick green potion that bubbled away over a fire. Another was lined with shelves full of dusty old books of magic spells. But there was no sign of the tsarina's hand mirror.

"I don't know about you, Rosie, but I'm completely lost!" Anastasia sighed, as they entered yet another corridor of mirrors. "I'm beginning to think Baba Yaga hasn't got any small mirrors at all!"

"We know she has your mother's hand mirror," Rosie replied. "We just have to find it." She glanced down at her cloak. Half of it had unravelled already. "And quickly, before my wool runs out," she added with a frown.

"Where shall we go now?" asked Anastasia, looking around.

"Let's try this way," Rosie suggested, pointing down another corridor.

Anastasia didn't reply. Rosie turned to look at her, and was shocked to see that all the colour had drained from her friend's face.

"Baba Yaga!" Anastasia whispered, shaking

all over as she pointed at the mirror nearest
to them.

Rosie looked and then gave a gasp of
horror. She could see Baba Yaga clearly
reflected in the mirror, and she realized that
the witch must be standing in one of the
corridors ahead of them.

"If we can see *her* reflection," Anastasia
pointed out in a nervous whisper, "then that
means that if she looks in the right direction,
she'll be able to see *ours*!"

Chapter Eight

Rosie felt a shiver run down her spine. "Maybe we should hide," she hissed. "We could try to get behind that big mirror over there."

"But if we move, we might catch her eye," Anastasia muttered.

The two girls stood as still as statues, holding their breath. Rosie could see that Baba Yaga already looked younger. Her hair had turned from grey to a glossy black, and her face and hands were much less wrinkled. The magic spells made from Anastasia's tears were obviously working.

The girls watched as Baba Yaga admired herself one last time in the mirror. Then, to their relief, the witch turned away and headed off down the corridor without noticing them.

Rosie let out a huge sigh. "That was close!" she murmured.

"We'd better not go *that* way!" Anastasia said, pointing after Baba Yaga.

Instead, the girls took a corridor which led in the opposite direction. There was a large room at the end of the passage, and the heavy wooden door stood ajar. The girls peeped in cautiously.

Like the corridors, the room was full of mirrors, but there was also a large four-poster bed with black drapes, and a dressing table and wardrobe, both made of heavy dark wood.

"This must be Baba Yaga's bedroom," said

Anastasia. "Look at all her beauty creams!"

The two girls crossed over to the dressing table to take a closer look. The table top was crammed with potions and lotions, soaps and creams.

Suddenly, Anastasia gave a cry and sprang forwards. "Rosie!" she cried, pushing aside a little glass bottle. "This is my mother's hand mirror!" She snatched up a silver mirror, the back of which was embossed with delicate flowers and leaves.

"Great!" Rosie declared, beaming at her. "Now let's get out of here."

"As fast as we can," Anastasia agreed. "Look." She pointed at a clock ticking on the wall. "It's almost eleven o'clock, Rosie. We only have an hour to get back to the palace and try to break the spell!"

Anastasia slipped the hand mirror into her bag, and the two girls made for the door. Quickly, they went back through the maze of mirrors, with Rosie gathering up the red woollen thread as they ran.

"There's the tunnel that leads to the entrance," Rosie panted. "Not far now, Anastasia!"

The girls dashed down the tunnel towards the front door. But to their dismay, it was held shut by several solid iron bolts. They were so heavy and stiff, the girls had to heave and pull together to open them. At last, the final bolt slid back.

"Let's go!" Rosie whispered, dragging open

the door.

The girls slipped
outside together and
Anastasia ran towards
the trees, but something
made Rosie hesitate.

"What are you
doing?" Anastasia
hissed, stopping to wait
for Rosie.

Rosie bit her lip
thoughtfully. "I'm
sorry, Anastasia," she
said, "but if I don't do
this, Baba Yaga won't
be at the palace by
midnight and our plan
won't work." And, with

that, Rosie raised her hand and deliberately
knocked one of the hanging icicles.

There was a loud *clink* as it knocked against the one nearest to it, which then knocked against the one nearest to that. Before the frightened girls had time to move a single step, every icicle hanging from Baba Yaga's house was suddenly swinging wildly and clanking loudly to sound the alarm. The noise was deafening.

Anastasia gaped at Rosie in terror.

"Run!" Rosie yelled, and the two girls took off, as fast as their legs could carry them, through the forest.

Rosie's heart was thumping madly in her chest as they headed back towards the river. It was hard to run because the trees were so close together that their branches kept catching at Rosie's hair like claws. Behind her she could hear the yapping of dogs and Baba Yaga screeching with rage.

"Come back!" yelled the witch. "You won't

escape me!"

Panting,
the two girls
reached the
riverbank and sat
down to put on
their skates. It had
started snowing again,
and great snowflakes
were drifting down from the
sky. Rosie was trembling so much, she was
all fingers and thumbs, but at last their skates
were on, and the girls sped away down the
frozen river at top speed.

As they skated away from the forest, the
yapping of dogs seemed to grow louder.
Rosie glanced back over her shoulder and
was horrified to see Baba Yaga speeding
along the ice in a sleigh drawn by eight
snarling black dogs.

"She's behind us, Anastasia," gasped Rosie. "And she's getting closer!"

"Skate faster!" Anastasia shouted.

Rosie tried to speed up, but she missed a step. Her feet seemed to get all tangled up with each other, and with a gasp of horror, she tumbled over.

Chapter Nine

"Rosie!" Anastasia cried. With the growling dogs snapping at their heels, Anastasia hauled Rosie to her feet, and the girls skated away again. But Baba Yaga was now closer than ever.

"Are you all right?" Anastasia asked anxiously.

"I'm fine!" Rosie panted. "Hurry!"

The girls could now see the frozen lake and the palace in front of them. Breathing hard, they skated to the edge of the lake, tore off their skates and grabbed their shoes. Baba Yaga's sleigh was heading towards them. She was so close now that Rosie could see the witch's fiery red eyes.

"You won't get away," she snarled, as she pulled the dogs to a halt. "I'm coming to get you!"

Rosie and Anastasia turned and fled towards the palace. They ran through the open French windows and into the ballroom. There, panting heavily, they looked up at the grandfather clock.

"Five to midnight!" Anastasia gasped. "Rosie, I hope your plan works."

"So do I," Rosie murmured, just as Baba Yaga appeared in the doorway.

Rosie and Anastasia huddled together as the witch advanced on them menacingly.

"So, Princess," Baba Yaga said, staring down her long nose at Anastasia, "you thought you could sneak into my house without permission, did you? And who are *you*?" she added, glaring at Rosie.

"I'm Anastasia's friend," Rosie replied bravely, staring Baba Yaga right in the eye.

Baba Yaga chuckled. "In that case you can give me your tears too!" She stroked her chin thoughtfully. "Or perhaps I'll turn you to ice. If Anastasia doesn't have any friends at all, then she will be sad and lonely and that will make her cry even more tears!" She laughed loudly, turning to Anastasia as she took the tiny bottle from her sleeve. "It's only a few minutes to midnight," she pointed out nastily, "and then it will be Christmas Day and my spell will become permanent. Your family and friends will be frozen for all eternity!"

As Baba Yaga stared eagerly at Anastasia, waiting for her to cry, Rosie stepped forwards. "It's not midnight *yet*," she said. "And if Anastasia can show you two snowflakes that look exactly the same, you promised that the spell would be broken."

"Oh, *yes*," Baba Yaga cackled. "I'd quite forgotten. Well?" She put her hands on her hips, a smirk on her lips. "*Can* you show me two identical snowflakes?"

Rosie nudged Anastasia. "Give me the mirror," she whispered.

Anastasia opened the bag and handed the mirror to Rosie.

Baba Yaga's red eyes narrowed with rage when she saw it. "That's mine!" she howled. "Give it to me!"

But Rosie gently took one of her own red curls and shook it over the mirror's surface. A large snowflake drifted down onto the glass.

"There," Rosie said, holding the mirror out to Baba Yaga. "Two snowflakes that look identical in every way!"

Baba Yaga stared at the snowflake and its reflection in the mirror.

"No!" she breathed, clutching her face. "NOOO!" she wailed as she looked up at the grandfather clock. For, at that moment, the clock began to chime the midnight hour.

The first chime was followed by a loud *crack* as the ice in the palace began to splinter and melt.

"Rosie, your plan has worked!" Anastasia cried joyfully.

"NOOO!" Baba Yaga screamed again, staring around the ballroom with her fierce red eyes. But chips of ice were already crashing to the floor all around her, and water was running down the walls and dripping from the hands of the grandfather clock.

Baba Yaga clutched at her hair. "My spell is broken!" she moaned in horror as she gazed around the palace. "My power is fading!"

Chapter Ten

Suddenly, music filled the ballroom. The musicians had started to play again, as the ice continued to melt. Here and there, people standing on the floor were beginning to dance, as if they had never stopped.

Rosie looked on with delight as more and more people slowly came back to life around her.

Then Anastasia gave a cry of joy. "Mama! Papa!"

Rosie watched as Anastasia dashed across the ballroom and flung herself into her mother's arms. The tsar and tsarina looked slightly confused, but apart from that, they seemed none the worse for their ordeal. Rosie smiled to herself. It was going to be a happy Christmas for Anastasia after all.

Looking round, Rosie noticed that Nikolai, the court magician, was also waking up. And as he did so, the frozen lightning-bolt of magic at the tip of

his wand seemed to wake up too, for it flew in a shining silver streak straight towards Baba Yaga.

The lightning-bolt whipped around the witch, lifting her off her feet. Then it swept her up and out of the palace. Rosie ran to the window to watch as the silver lightning whizzed through the night sky, taking Baba Yaga with it. She was howling with rage, but her screams faded away as the lightning carried her out of sight into the Great Forest.

"Your Majesty!" Nikolai announced, turning to the tsar. "My magic has banished Baba Yaga from the palace, and sent her back to her house, where she will be imprisoned for ever!"

The courtiers cheered.

"My friends," said the tsar, stepping forward with one arm around Anastasia and the other around his wife. "Baba Yaga is defeated. Now, at last, we can continue to celebrate Christmas and the engagement of my son, Prince Alexei, and his bride-to-be, Irina."

The courtiers clapped and cheered again as Anastasia's brother stood up and bowed. While they were applauding, Anastasia tugged at her father's sleeve and whispered in his ear. Then she hurried over to Rosie and took her hand.

"Papa, Mama," she said. "This is my friend, Rosie. It's thanks to her that the spell was broken. I could *never* have done it without her!"

Rosie blushed and curtseyed as Anastasia's father took her hand.

"Thank you for all your help, my dear," he

said gently. "You will always be an honoured guest at my royal palace."

"Thank you," Rosie said with a smile.

"Now let us celebrate!" the tsar called.

Immediately, the musicians struck up a merry tune and everyone began to dance. Rosie looked around happily, delighted to see the once silent, frozen ballroom now alive with colour and movement, and filled with the sounds of laughter and music. She longed to stay and join the fun, but she knew it was time for her to go home.

"Anastasia," Rosie whispered, taking her friend's arm and leading her out through the French windows into the garden. "I have to go home now, so that I can spend Christmas with my own family."

"Of course," Anastasia agreed. "But you *will* come back and visit me, won't you?"

"I'd love to!" Rosie exclaimed. "I need to

practise my ice-skating!"

Anastasia laughed and gave Rosie a hug.

"Goodbye!" Rosie said, waving
cheerfully at her new
friend as a snowy
whirlwind
sprang up
and swept
her gently
off her feet.

Rosie closed
her eyes as she
felt herself being
carried swiftly
through the air.
A moment later,
she felt her feet
touch solid
ground
again.

She opened her eyes and blinked. She was back in the dining room at the castle, standing in front of the table. The six Russian dolls were lined up in front of her, and Rosie could see that the little princess was now smiling.

"I've finished tidying my room, and it only took five minutes!" Luke declared, bursting into the dining room, looking very pleased with himself. "What are those?" he added, pointing to the dolls.

"They're Russian dolls," Rosie explained. "Look, they come apart and fit neatly inside each other."

Luke rushed over to take a closer look. "They're really cool," he said, picking up the tsar. "Who are they?"

"That's the tsar," Rosie explained. "He's King of Russia. And this is his wife, the tsarina. And this one—"

"Is a magician!" Luke interrupted excitedly.

Rosie nodded. "And there's a warrior and a prince and then there's the smallest doll of all." She picked it up and held it out for Luke to see. "This is the Snowflake Princess!" she told him. "See how she's smiling?"

Luke peered at the tiny doll. "I wonder why she's so happy?" he said thoughtfully. Then he grinned. "Maybe it's because it's Christmas!" Rosie laughed. "Yes, everyone loves Christmas," she agreed. *And this one's going to be the best ever!* she added to herself, smiling at the little princess in her hand.

THE END

Did you enjoy reading about Rosie's
adventures with the Snowflake Princess?
If you did, you'll love the next
Little Princesses
book!

Turn over to read the first chapter
of *The Dream-catcher Princess*.

Chapter One

Chapter One

Rosie Campbell stood at the entrance to the maze in the grounds of the castle and grinned at her younger brother. "Fancy a race?" she asked him.

Luke nodded eagerly. "Last one out the other side has to tidy the other's bedroom!"

Rosie laughed at the cheeky look on Luke's face. Her little brother was always looking for ways to get out of doing his chores. "Well, OK," she said teasingly, "if you're sure you want to tidy my bedroom. On your marks . . . get set . . . go!"

The two charged into the maze, Luke bearing off to the left and Rosie taking the right-hand path. They'd both been through the enormous hedge maze lots of times before, but neither of them knew the quickest way around it yet.

The sound of Luke's voice had faded into the distance and, as Rosie looked around, she realized that all she could see was the blue sky above and the high privet hedges on either side of her. Frost crunched on the path beneath her feet as she hurried round a corner and found herself in the centre of the maze. And there, in the middle, was one of Great-aunt Rosamund's most treasured possessions: the totem pole.

Despite being in the middle of a race, Rosie couldn't resist stopping for a closer look. The totem pole was a towering wooden post, intricately carved and brightly painted in shades of black, red, white, turquoise, green and yellow. It was five times the height of Rosie and so thick that Rosie couldn't quite touch her own fingertips when she put her arms around it.

Wow! thought Rosie, running her fingers over the weathered wood. She remembered her great-aunt telling her that the Native American Indians used totem poles as a way of recording stories. Every carving on the pole represented another part of the overall story.

Rosie gazed at the carvings, wondering what the tale of this particular pole was. There were many figures carved, one on top of the other, including an owl, an eagle, a star and a creature that looked like a playful dog. For the first time, Rosie noticed a carving of a girl on horseback. She looked closely at her. The girl was staring into the distance with a determined look on her face and she wore a pretty beaded circlet around her head.

Rosie's heart quickened. "Could this be

another little princess?" she wondered aloud. There was only one way to find out!

Rosie dropped into a curtsey. "Hello," she whispered to the girl on the horse. The word had barely left her lips when a gust of wind swirled around Rosie, and she could suddenly smell the fresh, sharp tang of pine trees.

Rosie jumped as somebody suddenly grabbed her arm and dragged her to the ground. "Hey!" she gasped in surprise.

A full moon slid out from behind a cloud, looking like a shiny silver coin in the sky. By its light, Rosie could see that she had been pulled down behind a large boulder by a girl who looked very similar to the figure on the totem pole. The girl looked at Rosie and held a warning finger to her lips.

Rosie nodded and then cautiously peeped round the edge of the boulder to see what they were hiding from. At first, she couldn't see anything at all, but as she stared into the darkness she began to make out three shadowy shapes only metres away. Her skin prickled with goosebumps as she realized that they were hideous-looking monsters.

One of the monsters was enormous, with six or seven thick legs, and long feelers stretching out from its head. Another was smaller and more octopus-shaped. It squirmed along on a mass of tentacles and made a soft squelching sound as it moved. The third monster looked like an overgrown cockroach. It scuttled busily this way and that, its legs making horrible clicking noises and its antennae wiggling furiously.

Rosie kept completely still as she watched, her heart pounding. She hardly dared to breathe. The monsters all seemed to be looking for something – or someone. Were they hunting for the princess?

Rosie nervously withdrew behind the rock because the monsters were drawing closer and closer. Looking up, she could just see the largest monster's feelers appearing over the top of the boulder and hear it making low gulping sounds. Do the monsters want to eat us? Rosie wondered.

Then, abruptly, the monsters and the noises stopped. Rosie bit her lip nervously. Where had the monsters gone? Somehow the eerie silence was even worse than the gulping noises.

The princess gently nudged her and pointed at the sky. Rosie looked up and realized that the sun was starting to rise. Streaks of orange light were spreading slowly into the dark blue of the night. As the sun rose higher and its rays glanced off the boulder, the little princess cautiously peeped over the top of the rock. Rosie did the same and saw that the monsters had completely vanished.

"They've gone," the princess said in a relieved voice. "Thank goodness!" she added, as she stood up and stretched in the sunshine.

"What were they?" Rosie breathed.

"It's a long story," the princess sighed. Then she smiled. "I should probably introduce myself first. My name is Princess Malila."

Read the rest of *The Dream-catcher Princess* to follow Rosie's adventures!